Craftily EVER AFTER

- - Best Buds Forever - -

By Martha Maker **Illustrated by Xindi Yan**

LITTLE SIMON

New York London Toronto Sydney New Delhi

LITTLE SIMON

An imprint of Simon & Schuster Children's Publishing Division
1230 Avenue of the Americas, New York, New York 10020
First Little Simon hardcover edition May 2020
Copyright © 2020 by Simon & Schuster, Inc.
For information about special discounts for bulk purchases, please contact Simon & Schuster
Special Sales at 1-866-506-1949 or business@simonandschuster.com.
The Simon & Schuster Speakers Bureau can bring authors to your live event. For
more information or to book an event contact the Simon & Schuster Speakers Bureau
at 1-866-248-3049 or visit our website at www.simonspeakers.com.
Series design by Laura Roode
Book design by Leslie Mechanic
The text of this book was set in Caecilia.
Manufactured in the United States of America 0320 FFG
2 4 6 8 10 9 7 5 3 1
Cataloging-in-Publication Data is available for this title from the Library of Congress.
ISBN 978-1-5344-6355-4 (hc)
ISBN 978-1-5344-6354-7 (pbk)
ISBN 978-1-5344-6356-1 (eBook)

CONTENTS

What Garden?

Tweet! Tweet! Tweet!

"Emily, look who's here again." Sam pointed at the bird, which had flown in through the window of the craft clubhouse—formerly known as the old shed in Bella's backyard. Emily Adams, Sam Sharma, Bella Diaz, and Maddie Wilson spent as much time as possible at the clubhouse.

Emily looked up from the wood piece she was sanding. "Hey, little guy," she greeted the bird. Emily turned to Maddie. "Why do you think he keeps coming back?"

"Maybe he's hungry," said Maddie.

"Or maybe," suggested Bella, "he heard about the birdhouse Emily made for her dad. He's here to ask her for blueprints."

"Don't you mean *bluebird* prints?" joked Maddie.

"Want to make another one?" Sam asked Emily.

"Maybe," said Emily. The first one had been a lot of work, but also a lot of fun. Maybe there was a different kind of birdhouse she could make this time.

Knock! Knock!

It was Bella's dad
knocking on the
doorframe of the
open clubhouse
door. He had a
big platter in
his arms.

"Now, that's
the *proper* way
to come into the
clubhouse," joked
Bella, nodding
at the bird. Her
friends laughed.

"Wow, what are those?" asked Sam, pointing to the platter. Since Mr. Diaz was a chef, he often tried out new recipes on Bella and her friends. But this looked less like food and more like . . .

"Flowers?" guessed Maddie.

Bella's dad nodded. "Squash blossoms. I harvested them this morning, then stuffed them and roasted them. Try for yourself!"

"Are you sure?" asked Sam. "My little sister tried to eat a flower once. Luckily, my mom stopped her just in time."

"Some flowers aren't good to eat," agreed Mr. Diaz. "But squash blossoms are edible. . . ."

"And delicious!" said Bella, digging in. The others did the same and quickly agreed.

"Mr. Diaz, what did you mean when you said you harvested them?" asked Emily.

"From our garden," he explained.

The kids looked at one another. "What garden?" asked Sam. They had spent many happy hours in the Diaz family's backyard—if there was a garden, surely they would have seen it.

Mr. Diaz laughed. "It's on the other side of the house. Technically, it's on our neighbor's property, but we worked out a deal. I tend the garden, and he enjoys some of what I grow."

"He grows *everything*," said Bella proudly.

Mr. Diaz laughed. "Come see for yourselves. Follow me!"

CHAPTER 2

An Idea Takes Root

Emily was at the kitchen table doing her homework. Or *trying* to, at least. She couldn't stop thinking about the Diaz family's garden. Vegetables, fruit, flowers: everything was fresh and flourishing, right there in the dirt. She doodled a curly pumpkin vine in her notebook and was adding leaves when something her dad said caught her attention.

"Did you just say 'garden'?" Emily asked her parents, who were in the living room.

Emily's mom turned, surprised. "Your dad was talking about that empty lot on Oak Street. It used to be a community garden."

"But now it's just an 'eyesore,' according to some people," explained Mr. Adams, who was on the town board. "At last night's meeting, we heard lots of complaints."

"Maybe it should go back to being a community garden," suggested Emily.

Her dad sighed. "It's not that simple. The mayor wants to get a store to open there. He thinks it could help the local economy."

Emily frowned. "What does that mean?"

"Local businesses help our town," explained Emily's mom. "They bring people together. And they pay taxes to the town. That money can go toward things like summer concerts and recycling pickup."

"But what about a good garden?" asked Emily. "Gardens bring people together. Plus, gardens produce all sorts of things: flowers and food."

Her dad nodded. "I agree. But it's up to the mayor, not me."

"Then I'll just have to talk to the mayor!" announced Emily.

Let's Get This Garden Started!

During library time at school the next day, Emily told Bella, Sam, and Maddie about the community garden—or what it *used* to be.

They all agreed that trying to rebuild the garden was a great idea.

"But we need the mayor's permission," explained Emily.

"Mayor Barnstable?" Maddie smiled. "He'll be glad to see us. We designed his favorite shirt, remember?"

"Um, we *tie-dyed* his shirt by *accident*," Sam reminded her.

"True. But he ended up loving it!" Maddie said, still smiling.

"That doesn't mean he'll automatically say yes to this," said Emily. "We'll need to convince him. We'll have to explain why a community garden is a good idea."

"Why don't we look online?" suggested Bella.

The others gathered around and suggested search terms while Bella typed. Just "gardens" got too many results, but adding the word "community" narrowed them down.

"Ooh, an article about the many benefits of community gardens," read Maddie. "Click on that link."

Sam sat down next to Bella and pulled out his sketch pad. He took notes while Bella scrolled through information. Meanwhile, Emily and

Maddie looked for books about gardening.

"Did you get the part about photosynthesis?" Bella asked Sam.

"Of course." Sam showed her his sketch of a happy plant absorbing harmful CO_2 molecules from the air and releasing valuable oxygen molecules *into* the air.

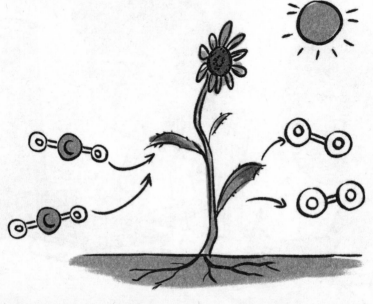

"Awesome," said Bella. "Can you add some birds? According to this site, gardens provide them with habitats, and they eat tiny critters that can destroy plants and crops."

"Absolutely," said Sam.

"Bugs!" yelled Bella, causing Sam to jump. She laughed and pointed to the screen, then whispered, "Look! Insects help gardens too."

Before long, Bella had printed out several pages of facts, Sam had filled his notebook with notes and drawings, and Maddie and Emily had checked out a stack of gardening books.

They were ready to get this garden started. Or ready to *start* to get this garden started.

Door to Door

On Saturday morning, Emily went to temple with her family. Emily always tried to pay attention to the rabbi, but she couldn't help daydreaming sometimes. Like she was doing right now. Suddenly, a word brought her back to focus.

Gan? Did Rabbi Stein just say the Hebrew word for "garden"?

Sure enough, the rabbi said it again. "When we talk about 'healing the world,' there are lots of things you can do that are very small, yet very important," she explained to everyone. "Planting seeds, growing vegetables or flowers, and sharing them with others are all ways to heal the world . . . even if your *gan* is just a single flowerpot."

Or *a single vacant lot*, thought Emily excitedly.

That afternoon, Emily's friends came over. She greeted them with happy news.

"The mayor agreed to meet with us!" she told them. "Thursday after school."

Everyone cheered. Then they got down to business. They had decided that a petition would be a good place to start. They'd go around Emily's neighborhood, explain the benefits of a community garden, and then ask people if they'd like to sign the petition. Emily's next-door neighbor was up first.

When Mrs. Simms heard about the community garden, she smiled broadly. "What a terrific idea. Where do I sign?"

Within the very first hour, they knocked on twelve doors and collected—

"Twelve signatures!" announced Maddie.

"Let's go get lucky number thirteen," said Emily, leading the way.

When a man answered the door, the kids launched into their now-well-rehearsed pitch. Sam held up a poster they had made with all their facts—and drawings that illustrated the facts. Emily described the information on the poster, and Sam showcased a proposed garden map.

The man stared at the map. Then he said, "Is there any chance you

kids might like some plant donations for your garden? I run a plant
nursery, so I know how important
gardens can be. And your presenta-
tion covers it all!"

"Wow! That would be amazing.
Thank you!" said Emily.

By the time they returned to Emily's house, they had two full pages of signatures. And just as amazing—they had received more offers of donations and help, too!

They'd been offered compost, credit at a local flower shop, bags of mulch, and even a beehive.

Of course the kids had told
everyone that the community garden wasn't a done deal, but now
Emily couldn't help but feel that it
just *had* to become a reality.

CHAPTER 5

Maddie's Surprise

The week practically flew by. Every day, Emily and her friends met after school at one of their houses and then "canvassed" the neighborhood—Mr. Adams told them that was what knocking on doors with a petition was called.

"Amazing! One hundred signatures!" shouted Sam on Wednesday

afternoon when the last door closed.

"Wow! That's going to impress the mayor for sure," said Bella.

"Let's get back to the clubhouse," suggested Maddie. "We've got work to do!"

"Let me guess," said Sam. "You want to figure out what we're going to wear to our meeting?"

"Possibly," said Maddie with a smile.

At the clubhouse, Maddie pulled out rolls of fabric. "Let's see," she said. "Green for growing things. That will suit you, Bella. Brown for the earth and branches and tree bark. Hold this, Emily. Yellow for . . ."

"Me!" Sam called, making everyone laugh. Yellow was Sam's favorite color.

"And I'll take blue for water,"
Maddie concluded. "Our signature
ensembles are going to rock!"

"Maddie," said Emily gently, "you're a sewing whiz. But our meeting is tomorrow after school. Even if you stayed up all night, it would be impossible to make four outfits from scratch."

"We could help you," said Bella. "Except I kind of wanted to turn our statistics into graphs."

"I was going to redo our poster to make it look more polished," said Sam.

"And I was going to write a script," said Emily. "My dad said it's a really good way to organize thoughts and stay on topic."

Maddie looked a little disappointed.

"Hang on," said Bella.

She ran out of the clubhouse and into her house. She returned with a bag, which she handed to Maddie.

Maddie peeked inside, squealed, and gave Bella a hug. Then she gathered up all the material and ran to her sewing machine.

"These won't be ready in time for the meeting with the mayor, but they'll come in handy once he approves our plans, for sure!" Maddie announced.

"What did you give her?" asked Emily.

"You'll see," said Bella. "Now, let's all get to work—our big meeting is tomorrow!"

CHAPTER
6

Meeting with the Mayor

The next afternoon, Emily's mom accompanied Emily and her friends on their trip to Mayor Barnstable's office.

When they arrived, the mayor's secretary told them, "The mayor says he has a very important meeting scheduled."

"He does?" Emily's face fell.

"Does that mean we have to wait until it is over?"

The secretary shook his head and smiled. "The important meeting is with you four."

"Oh!" The four friends gathered up their papers and nervously shuffled into the mayor's office.

"Well, if it isn't my very favorite designers," said Mayor Barnstable. "I can't tell you how many compliments I get when I wear the shirt that you kids, uh, *crafted* for me."

"Thanks!" said Maddie, giving an encouraging look to Emily.

Emily took a long, deep breath and then stepped forward. "Mayor Barnstable," she said, "thank you for agreeing to meet with us. My friends and I have an idea for revitalizing the vacant lot over on Oak Street."

"Revitalizing?" asked the mayor.

"Yes," said Emily. "It means making it healthier and more useful.

Many years ago, that lot was a community garden. Our idea is to return it to its former glory, so that people of all ages can come together to grow flowers and vegetables. The garden would also be a place for relaxation. And events like concerts and craft festivals could be held there too."

"Do you think the community would support it?" asked the mayor.

"We do," said Bella, producing a graph. "We canvassed several neighborhoods and got a hundred signatures on our petition. And many of those who signed offered to make donations or volunteer."

"And we made a garden map," said Sam, showing the mayor his drawing. "To show how we might use the site." Sam's dad, an architect, had shown Sam and his friends how to use a special ruler called a scale to make sure the map was accurate.

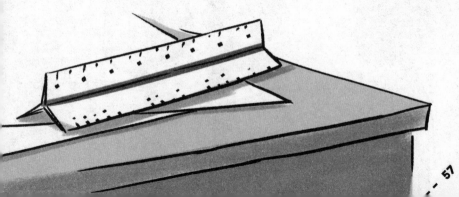

"Very interesting," said the mayor. "I do have some questions, if you don't mind."

Emily, Bella, Sam, and Maddie exchanged a quick look of concern.

Fortunately, it turned out that the kids had answers to all of the mayor's questions, but the easiest one of all was the question of who would lead the project if it moved forward. It would be all four of them.

CHAPTER 7

Is No News Bad News?

"Emily! Any word from the mayor?" called Mrs. Simms when she saw Emily and her mom at the library.

Emily shook her head sadly. When the meeting with the mayor ended, he said he would be in touch. But he didn't say when.

Mrs. Simms patted Emily on

the shoulder. "I'm sure you'll hear soon," she said.

Emily nodded, trying to look confident. It had been a whole week. What was taking so long?

Later that afternoon, Emily went to the craft clubhouse. As soon as she walked in, everyone turned to look at her.

"Any news?" her friends all asked at once.

Emily threw her hands up in exasperation. "You guys! Don't you think I would tell you if I heard something?"

"Sorry," said Bella. "I'm just having a hard time thinking about anything else."

"Me too!" said Sam.

"We need a new project to take our minds off the garden," agreed Maddie.

The four friends sat in silence. Each of them tried to think of a new craft idea that wasn't related to gardens.

Knock! Knock!

"Hey, maybe your dad harvested some more of those squash blossoms," said Maddie.

But instead of Bella's dad, it was Emily's mom.

"What's up?" asked Emily.

"I just got a call from the mayor," explained Mrs. Adams. "He asked to speak to you and said it was important. I said if he called back shortly, I could put you on the phone. Then I came straight here."

Mrs. Adams's cell phone rang. "That's him now," she said, handing the phone to Emily.

"Hello?" said Emily nervously. "Uh-huh. Got it. Sure. Okay." Emily's friends gathered around her, trying to read her face for clues. *Good news? Bad news?*

"Thank you," Emily finally said. "Bye."

Emily handed the phone back.

Emily's eyes closed. Her head dropped. Her hands balled into fists.

Noooo, thought Sam, Bella, and Maddie.

"Yessss!"

Emily's friends watched as she jumped triumphantly, head held high, fists in the air.

"So he approved the idea?" asked Maddie.

Emily beamed and nodded. "And not only that, but he's also going to get his team to prepare the soil and everything so we can start planting right away!"

"Yessss!" everyone let out a huge cheer, together this time.

CHAPTER 8

SOIL

Breaking Ground

A few weeks later, the friends arrived at the vacant lot in town. They were pleased to see that the mayor had fulfilled his promise. There were piles of prepared soil, as well as wheelbarrows, shovels, trowels, hoses, watering cans, and even some sets of gardening gloves.

Plus, the four friends had brought supplies of their own.

"Garden markers, check!" called Maddie, holding up bags of wooden craft sticks and pens.

"Garden benches, check!" added Emily, who was grateful to have her dad to assist with moving the garden furniture she and her friends had built.

"The aprons Maddie made, check!" said Bella. That day in the clubhouse, Bella had gone back to her house to get extra canvas aprons her dad had lying around. And Maddie had totally blinged them out! Each apron had a kid's name on it, plus a cool garden-related design.

The friends could use the pockets
for gardening tools as they worked!

"Garden plans, check, check,
check!" Sam chimed in, handing
out copies of the map to volunteers
as they started to arrive. Maddie
ran around with a clipboard, wel-
coming them.

Many of the volunteers were people who had signed the petition. Some had brought things to donate: seeds, pots, tools, and more. Bella, who had brought her tablet, kept a running tally of donated items.

After they finished volunteer check-in, the four friends spread out and manned their stations. Emily led a team of volunteers as they measured and marked out the main planting beds.

Bella's team kept preparing the soil. Maddie's team cut the grass and trimmed plants. And Sam's team

organized supplies and distributed them throughout the garden.

The morning flew by as they dug, rearranged, and planted. Since Bella loved to do research, she was in charge of fielding all questions that came up. Questions like: "Is this a plant we should keep, or is it a weed?"

Bella quickly searched online. "Keep!"

"What about this one?" asked Mrs. Simms. "Full sun, partial sun, or shade?"

"Full sun!" said a voice.

Bella looked up. It was Mayor Barnstable. "That's lavender," he said with a smile. "It was my mother's favorite plant. She always said lavender needs a lot of sun."

The next thing Bella knew, the mayor was rolling up his sleeves, digging in the dirt, and carefully placing the lavender plant. He watered it, then patted the soil to ensure the little plant took root.

Bella smiled at him.

The mayor cleaned off his hands, then gathered the volunteers.

"I want to thank you all for help- ing to revitalize this lot," he said. Then he gestured at Emily, Maddie, Bella, and Sam. "And I really want to thank four outstanding young community members for their inspiration and determination."

As the crowd cheered, the four friends beamed. Then they refilled their water bottles and got back to work. They had a garden to build!

The Garden Grows!

All week, the friends worked on the garden. Each day after school they turned soil, repotted plants, and watered seedlings. At the end of the week, most of what they planted still needed time to grow, but the garden was definitely taking shape.

"Looks great, kids."

Emily turned to see the mayor, who had come to check on their progress.

"I can hardly believe this is the same lot," he added. "In fact, there's only one thing this garden still really needs. And I'm afraid it can't open to the public without it."

The friends looked at each other nervously. Had they forgotten to file some important paperwork?

"Wh-what's that?" asked Emily.

The mayor's serious face slowly shifted into a grin. "A party!" he announced.

"Like with music and games and cake?" asked Sam.

"And crafts?" suggested Maddie.

The mayor laughed. "Yes, of course! Your creativity is the reason the garden is here in the first place. You kids should definitely take the lead in making the opening day of the garden a celebration of creativity and community!"

"Sounds great!" said Emily. Her friends nodded excitedly.

"Everyone will be invited," continued the mayor. "We should probably do it in a few months, so we can show off the bounty that the garden has produced." The mayor clapped his hands together. "This is going to be a celebration to remember!"

After the mayor said good-bye,
Emily, Maddie, Bella, and Sam gathered up their tools and turned off
the sprinklers.

Then, before they went home,
they stood quietly in the beautiful
space.

"This garden is magical," said Sam. Maddie nodded.

"I love how peaceful it is," added Bella.

"Me too," said Emily. "Hang on. . . . Do you hear that?"

The others were silent. Then the sound came again.

"Look!" said Emily, pointing.

Sure enough, it was a little bird. It circled around the garden, then landed on a green bush.

Emily smiled. Her friends, the mayor, and now this little bird had given her an awesome idea.

"Ah! Home sweet clubhouse," sang Maddie as the four friends gathered around the big worktable again.

They had spent so many weeks working on the garden that it actually felt a little strange to be indoors. But now the grand opening of the garden was only a couple months

away, and the kids still needed to figure out which crafts they'd each be leading at the party.

"I have an idea," said Maddie. "Remember those wood craft sticks we used to show which veggies were planted where? Take a look at these."

Maddie pulled out a handful of felt shapes. One was purple, one was orange, another was red, and the final one was green. "Eggplant, carrot, tomato, and peas," she explained. "We just glue them onto the sticks, and they'll do the same job, only craftier!"

"Cool!" said Sam. "I also had an idea for an upgrade. Remember those stepping-stones we positioned in the flower beds? Well, check these out."

He opened his backpack and pulled out a pair of small rocks. But when he flipped them over . . .

"Ladybugs!" exclaimed Bella. Sure enough, Sam had painted both rocks bright red, then added black spots and cheerful faces.

"Wouldn't it be cool if we painted the stepping-stones this way too?" asked Sam.

Bella nodded. "I have a craft idea as well." She called them over to her

computer and showed them examples online. "See? You take recycled materials, like the plastic lids from take-out containers. Then you cut out the centers and use colored tissue paper. Ta-da! Suncatchers."

"Those are so awesome," said Maddie. "And I love how they're made out of things people might otherwise throw away!"

"What about you, Emily?" asked Bella. "Do you have a craft idea for the party?"

Emily smiled. "The little bird we saw gave me an idea," she said. Just then, the same bird that had visited them in the clubhouse before flew in. "And I think *this* little bird will like it too!" Emily added with a laugh. Her friends would just have to wait and see.

Best Buds Forever

Over the next couple of months, the friends visited the garden regularly. They watered, weeded, and took photographs and measurements. Every day brought exciting new developments.

"Guys, look! These vines have flowering buds," called Sam one day. A few weeks later, he pointed out the same plant. "The buds are now gone, and in their place are string beans!"

"Awesome," said Bella. "Check this out." The others joined her, expecting to look down at a growing plant.

Instead, they had to look up! "Wow, that sunflower is taller than you, Bella!"

Bella giggled. "I think it's even taller than the mayor."

Finally, the big day arrived. Emily's parents and Bella's parents helped the kids bring over a few craft supplies, some borrowed tables, and an assortment of delicious treats made by Mr. Diaz. A local bakery had provided cupcakes, and the coffee shop set up a stand serving coffee, tea, and lemonade. The jazz band and the chorus from the local high school, where Sam's mom taught, had agreed to perform. And the staff of the local animal shelter brought some adorable—and adoptable!—dogs.

"Now, *this* is a party!" announced Sam as the garden began to fill up with guests. From his crafting station, he waved to Emily, Maddie, and Bella. Each was busy teaching crafts to eager kids and community members.

Emily's craft turned out to be
bird feeders made out of milk car-
tons! With some snipping, gluing,
and painting, the feeders sprouted
wings and beaks, so they looked
like birds themselves!

Emily took a moment to look around at all the guests. There were so many people, young and old. She spotted Mrs. Simms, who was with her son and granddaughter. She saw their schoolteacher, Ms. Gibbons. Just then, someone tapped Emily on the shoulder.

"*Kol hakavod!* Well done, Emily!" It was Rabbi Stein, smiling at her. "You and your friends did a great job," added the rabbi. "This garden is truly amazing."

Emily thanked the rabbi for the compliment.

Tweet! Tweet! Tweet!

Emily glanced up and saw that a bird had landed on one of the completed milk-carton bird feeders.

"And thank you for the inspiration," she said to the little bird. The bird had been her inspiration for this craft project, but also, along with her friends, for her idea to create another wooden birdhouse that would live forever in the garden.

Emily looked over at it on its tall wooden posts and saw that a few different birds were enjoying it!

Just then, the mayor's assistant signaled that it was time for the official welcome speech.

"As many of you know," said Mayor Barnstable, "this location was once an abandoned lot. But then Emily, Maddie, Bella, and Sam came along. One of the things they said to me when they first came to my office was that this project would be good for the community. As we can all see today, they were one-hundred-percent right."

Emily smiled at her friends, family, and the many butterflies flying around. The garden *was* good for the community. It was good for individual people, like Rabbi Stein and Mrs. Simms and all the babies, kids, and adults who were there.

And it was good for the animals and plants who were enjoying their new home.

And it was also good for Emily and her friends. With all their creativity and hard work, they had proven that they could truly work as a team. Emily was certain that she, Maddie, Bella, and Sam would be best buds forever.

How to Make . . .
A Milk or Juice Carton Bird Feeder

What you need:

X-Acto knife
Milk or juice carton
Acrylic paint—or waterproof paint would be even better!
Paintbrush
Glue
Wood craft stick
Birdseed

Step I: With an X-Acto knife, cut an opening in the center of one side of the carton—this will be the opening for the birds to go into. Below that, make a small slit—this will be for the bird perch.

Have an adult help you with this step!

Step 2: Paint the carton any color and design you want!

Step 3:

Insert a wood craft stick into the slit you cut earlier. On the inside of the carton, add some glue so the craft stick stays put.

Step 4: Add birdseed to your feeder. Then place it outside for the birds to enjoy!

HEiDi HECKELBECK

EBOOK EDITIONS ALSO AVAILABLE
from LITTLE SIMON
simonandschuster.com/kids

the adventures of

SOPHIE MOUSE

EBOOK EDITIONS ALSO AVAILABLE
from LITTLE SIMON

simonandschuster.com/kids